Books by Robert Bright

The Friendly Bear
Georgie
Georgie and the Robbers
Georgie to the Rescue
Georgie's Halloween
I Like Red
Me and the Bears
My Hopping Bunny
Richard Brown and the Dragon
Which Is Willy?

Georgie and the Magician

by ROBERT BRIGHT

Doubleday & Company, Inc.
Garden City, New York

Library of Congress Catalog Card Number 66–10822
Copyright © 1966 by Robert Bright
Printed in the United States of America
All Rights Reserved
15   14   13   12   11

For Christopher

Georgie was the gentle little ghost who creaked the Whittakers' stairs and squeaked their parlor door and made everybody feel cozy and comfortable for the night.

But just because he was a ghost, Georgie never supposed he was especially magical.

Until one time when something special happened to Mr. Whittaker, and that was right after something special happened to the harmless cow in the meadow.

What happened to the cow was that her
barn caught fire.
Georgie saw the glow of the fire from his
attic window and warned Miss Oliver,
the owl, and she began to hoot to beat
the band.

Then he warned Herman, the cat, and
Herman woke up the Whittakers, and
Mr. Whittaker rushed out, pulling on
his volunteer fireman's uniform.

After that everybody got out to
the meadow as fast as he could.
But it wasn't fast enough.

The barn burned down.
Winter was coming on.
Where would the harmless cow live when the snow began to fall?
Well, there was only one thing to be done: build a new barn. And there was only one way to do it.

The village must give a COW BARN
BENEFIT ENTERTAINMENT at
the Town Hall to raise the money.
So that's what they decided to do there
and then. Miss Thompson said she'd
sing, Jimmy Holt said he'd fiddle, and
Mrs. Whittaker said she'd play the piano.
Mr. Whittaker said that HE would
entertain with MAGICAL TRICKS.

Now that would have been all right because Mr. Whittaker had done magic as a hobby once and he still had his magic kit packed away in the attic. So he knew a few tricks—little ones.

But first thing the paper came out, and the paper said that Mr. Whittaker was going to wave his wand and catch a pigeon out of nowhere.

Next the posters went up, and the posters showed Mr. Whittaker pulling a rabbit out of his hat.

But that wasn't all. Because at the Town Hall children from all over the county were buying tickets, and they were telling each other that Mr. Whittaker was going to say a magical word. And when he said this word, Mrs. Whittaker was going to float in the air—like a balloon.

16

Mr. Whittaker went right home to his attic and unpacked his magic kit. But when he waved his wand all he could catch was a surprised little spider.

And when he reached into his hat, all he could pull out was a tired old moth ball.

18

So he said magical words, but all that
floated was a chicken feather.

With that Mr. Whittaker became so worried about disappointing the children, he could no longer sleep properly. Sometimes he talked in his sleep. Once he even walked in his sleep.

That was a fine how-do-you-do!

Herman and Miss Oliver decided something would have to be done, and they both thought they could help Mr. Whittaker be more magical. But they knew that Georgie could help more than anybody—because he was a ghost, and a ghost was just naturally the most magical of all.

Georgie was such a shy little ghost he wasn't sure he was magical the least bit. But then he saw how night after night Mr. Whittaker was getting more and more worried. So Georgie promised to try.

And he did. Every night while Mr. Whittaker practiced magic in his parlor, Georgie and his friends practiced in the tree across the road. Only you could never tell just what they were up to because the clouds kept hiding the light of the moon. You could only guess.

There wasn't an empty seat in the Town Hall on the night of the COW BARN
BENEFIT ENTERTAINMENT. And when Miss Thompson sang and Jimmy
Holt fiddled and Mrs. Whittaker played the piano everybody clapped. But when
Mr. Whittaker came on they all stomped their feet, they were so excited.

Mr. Whittaker flourished his magic wand and tried not to look as worried as he felt. But he knew—Oh he knew!—that he wasn't about to catch a pigeon. And he didn't.

He caught Miss Oliver.
Now that was puzzling!

Mr. Whittaker reached into his hat. And he knew—Oh he knew!—that he wasn't about to pull out a rabbit. But he did better.

He pulled out Herman.

PROGRAM

ss Thompson
SONG
Jimmy Holt
VIOLIN
r& Whittaker
PIANO
~&~
WHITTAKER
MAGIC
~&~

Mr. Whittaker was so puzzled, he scratched his ear. So he didn't rightly see what was happening to his hat.

But when he saw it was gone, he was so surprised, he said, "OHH!"

At that everybody thought he had said the magic word and expected
Mrs. Whittaker to float. Only it wasn't she.

It was Georgie. And maybe if Mr. Whittaker hadn't been so busy looking in all the wrong places, he would have seen where his hat was going.

And maybe if everybody hadn't cheered so loud, Georgie wouldn't have been scared.

He was so scared, he floated out the window.

AND he kept on floating.

Georgie floated across the quiet Green, and that was already less scary—

Georgie floated up the main street, and that was hardly scary at all.

Georgie floated down the winding road, and that was easy.

Georgie floated all the way home, and he wished he didn't have to stop. It was such fun being magical!

But what a puzzle it was for Mr. Whittaker!

He had no idea what had made *him* magical. He began to wonder.

They had the new barn built before the first snow fell. And no one, not even the cow herself, was more pleased than Mr. Whittaker. Hadn't it been his magic that had made the BENEFIT such a success?

Still, he couldn't stop wondering how magically it had all happened.

He wondered about Miss Oliver. But Miss Oliver just winked.

He wondered about Herman. Herman just purred.

But mostly Mr. Whittaker wondered about what had become of his top hat.

One evening he climbed to the attic and found out.

Just the same Mr. Whittaker kept wondering.

Because who—WHO—had put it there?

WHO?

Robert Bright was born on Cape Cod, spent his childhood in Europe, and completed his education at Phillips Academy, Andover, and Princeton University.

His vocations include those of newspaper reporter in Baltimore and Paris, art and music critic in Santa Fe, New Mexico, teacher in Boston, and novelist. Believing that "the imaginative child in the imaginative man is fortunately never far away," Mr. Bright has delighted in writing and illustrating his fourteen books for children. Five of these star Georgie, the friendly little ghost who first appeared in 1944 and who has been charming young readers on both sides of the Atlantic ever since.

Robert Bright and his wife, Katherine, have their center in Santa Fe, but become nomadic during winters and springs. The happy stimulus for the earliest Georgie books furnished by their children, Beatrice and Robin, is now provided by two handy grandsons, Michael and Christopher.